BOOK TWO

More
Mr. and Mrs.
Green

KEITH BAKER

Harcourt, Inc.

Orlando   Austin   New York   San Diego   Toronto   London

For Laurie,
with great, green gratitude

Copyright © 2004 by Keith Baker

Requests for permission to make copies of any part of the work should be mailed to the following address: Permissions Department, Harcourt, Inc., 6277 Sea Harbor Drive, Orlando, Florida 32887-6777.

www.HarcourtBooks.com

First Harcourt paperback edition 2005

Library of Congress Cataloging-in-Publication Data
Baker, Keith.
More Mr. and Mrs. Green/Keith Baker.
p. cm.
Summary: Mr. and Mrs. Green, two alligators, spend time together fishing, painting, and going to the park.
[1. Fishing—Fiction. 2. Jellybeans—Fiction. 3. Painting—Fiction.
4. Parks—Fiction. 5. Alligators—Fiction.] I. Title.
PZ7.B17427Mo 2003
[E]—dc21 2002011385
ISBN 0-15-216494-4
ISBN 0-15-205246-1 (pb)

A C E G H F D B
A C E G H F D B (pb)

The illustrations in this book were done with acrylic paint on illustration board.
The display type was created by Jane Dill Design.
The text type was set in Giovanni Book.
Color separations by Colourscan Co. Pte. Ltd., Singapore
Printed and bound by Tien Wah Press, Singapore
Production supervision by Sandra Grebenar and Ginger Boyer
Designed by Keith Baker

Contents

Fishing

Mr. Green reeled in a fish.

"Another one!" he said.

"That makes 14.

I *love* fishing!"

Mrs. Green loved fishing, too—

only not today.

Today her pail was empty.

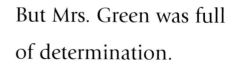

But Mrs. Green was full
of determination.

"Let's switch places," she said.
"All the fish are on *your*
side of the boat."

"Gladly," said Mr. Green.
(He liked fishing from either side.)

So they switched places.

The boat wobbled back and forth.

(Mr. Green almost fell in.)

They cast their lines out into the water.

Mrs. Green felt ready and steady—

she would catch the next fish.

But she didn't.

"Number 15," said Mr. Green.

"The biggest one yet!"

Mrs. Green had another idea.

"Let's trade fishing poles,"
she said.
"Your pole is shiny
and new."

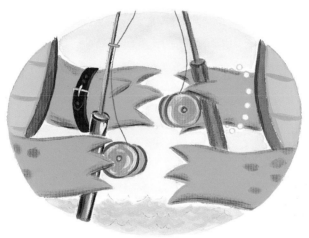

"With pleasure," said Mr. Green.
(He liked fishing with any pole.)

Mrs. Green felt ready
and steady and sure.

But not for long.

"Fan-fish-tas-tic!" said Mr. Green.

"Number 16!

8 + 8...4 x 4...½ of 32—

that's sixteen."

$8 + 8$ 16 $4 + 4$

$\frac{1}{2}$ of 32

"Oh, I do love fishing!" he said.

Mrs. Green was not
sharing his enthusiasm.
She felt frustrated
and fishless.

13

She had one more idea.

"May I wear your hat?
It must be lucky."

"Lucky?" asked Mr. Green.

"No, my lucky hat is at home."

"Then *how*," asked Mrs. Green,

"are you catching all those fish?"

"Jelly beans!" said Mr. Green.

"Gooey, chewy, yummy, gummy
jelly beans.
These fish love 'em."

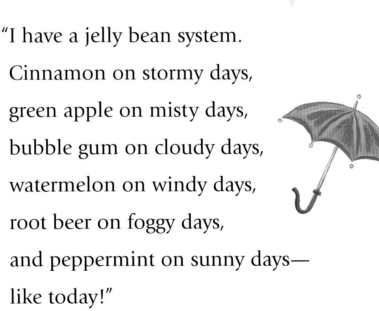

"I have a jelly bean system.
Cinnamon on stormy days,
green apple on misty days,
bubble gum on cloudy days,
watermelon on windy days,
root beer on foggy days,
and peppermint on sunny days—
like today!"

"And these licorice ones are good *any* time."

"Jelly bean?" asked Mr. Green.

"Peppermint, please," said Mrs. Green.

She slipped the jelly bean onto her hook.

She cast her line far out into the water.

She prepared herself for the catch, but…

…no nibbles…

…no bites…

…no fish.

Mr. Green was perplexed.

His system wasn't working.

Had the jelly bean slipped off?

Was it the wrong flavor?

Were the fish full?

Then all of a sudden, Mrs. Green felt

a tug and a jiggle,

then a wiggle and a yank.

"Jumping jelly beans," she shouted,
"I CAUGHT ONE!"

"Number 17!" said Mr. Green.

"And it's a beauty."

"Oh, I do love fishing," said Mrs. Green.

"I wonder…

…what we could catch with
chocolate chip cookies."

The Portrait

"I want to paint,"
said Mrs. Green.
"Something bright…
something bold…
something beautiful!"

"How about painting me?"

asked Mr. Green.

(He was not shy or modest.)

"Will you wear a tie?" asked Mrs. Green.

"Like always," said Mr. Green.

"Will you sit still?" asked Mrs. Green.

"Like a statue," said Mr. Green.

"Will you smile?" asked Mrs. Green.

"Like the Mona Lisa," said Mr. Green.

"And will you stay awake?" asked Mrs. Green.

"Like a night owl!" said Mr. Green.

But it was almost time for his nap.

Mr. Green selected

a colorful tie.

(He had 317 of them.)

He practiced smiling
in the mirror.
(He had a big smile,
with sparkly teeth.)

He pretended to be
a statue.
(He didn't move a
muscle or a bump
for 1 full minute.)

Then he pinched
himself—*ouch!*
He was wide awake.
His nap could wait.

Mr. Green sat down.

"Hold that pose!" said Mrs. Green.

She started painting at once—
she felt excited!
(Mr. Green *was* bright, bold,
and beautiful.)

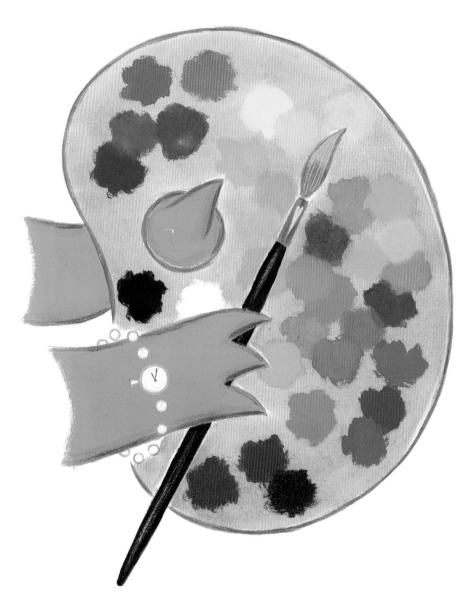

Mrs. Green mixed shades of every color—
especially green.

She observed all the shapes.

She studied all the shadows.

She did not miss a detail.

The hours flew by for her…

…but not for Mr. Green.

His nose tickled,

his foot itched,

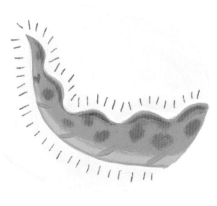

his tail tingled,

and his eyelids grew
heavier and
heavier and
heavier.

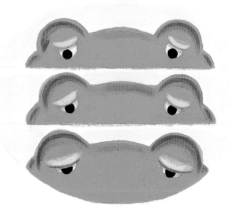

At last Mr. Green fell into
a deep, deep sleep.
It was a delicious sleep.
(He dreamt about pies.)

Mrs. Green could paint forever.

But she also knew when to stop.

"*Fini!*" she shouted at last.

(*Fini* means "finished" in French.)

Mr. Green was startled awake.

He had been napping for
2 hours, 36 minutes,
and 49 seconds.
Now it was time to see his portrait.

It was

It was

It was **Wild.**

Every humpy bump and speckly spot,

every sparkly tooth and pointy finger

were all there—

just jumbled up,

inside out,

flip-floppity.

Mr. Green was stunned.

And he was thrilled.

"It's me!" said Mr. Green.

"You've captured the real me.

It's spectacular.

It's stupendous.

It's *superb*."

(*Superb* means "superb" in French.)

Mrs. Green turned a little red.

She was embarrassed by all the compliments.

But she was also proud—proud as Picasso,

one of her favorite painters.

"Let's hang this in our gallery,"

said Mr. Green.

"I know just the place."

"It's another magnificent masterpiece," he said.

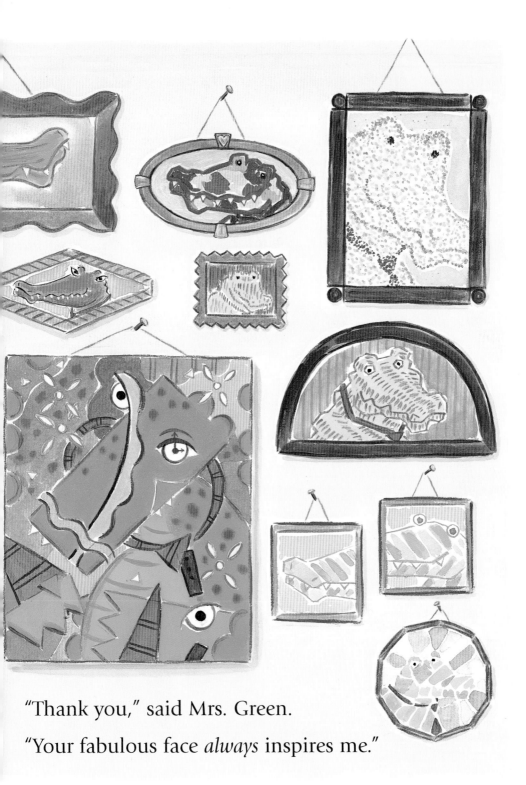

"Thank you," said Mrs. Green.

"Your fabulous face *always* inspires me."

At the Park

"I won, I won, I won!" said Mr. Green.

"First to the fountain."

He did a little victory dance.

Mrs. Green was not racing.

She was standing in the middle

of Emerald Garden.

"Look, look, look!" she said.

"So many butterflies—

graceful swallowtails…

magnificent monarchs…

glorious painted ladies…

They're dazzling!"

Mr. Green was not looking.

He was walking across
the monkey bars—
on his hands.
"Watch this!"

Mr. Green did a double
back flip onto the grass.
"A perfect 10!" he said.

Mrs. Green was not watching.

She was listening to the birds.

"So many songs!" said Mrs. Green.

"Robins warbling…

 sparrows chirping…

chickadees peeping…

It's like a symphony!"

Mr. Green was not listening.

He was swimming
back and forth
across the wading pool—
77 times.

"A new world record!"
said Mr. Green.
He raised his arms
in triumph.

Mrs. Green did not see him.

Her nose was in the flowers.

"*Ahhh…,*" she said.

"The sweet lilies…

the spicy daisies…

the perfumey roses…

They smell good enough to—"

Mrs. Green stopped.

She heard a sound.

She listened closely.

Mr. Green stopped.
He heard the
same sound.

It was one of their favorite sounds—

better than a cuckoo clock,

better than a train whistle,

even better than a marching band.

It was…

ding-a-ling ding ding ding

the bell on the ice-cream truck!

Mrs. Green looked at Mr. Green.

"First one there is the winner!" she said.

"Ready....Set....Go!"

They took off in a flash.

Mr. Green's stride was long—

for an alligator.

He pulled ahead.

Mrs. Green veered to the left.

She had a plan.

Mr. Green ran

under the rings,

around the merry-go-round,

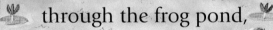

through the frog pond,

over the footbridge,

and down the final stretch.

But Mrs. Green was already there.
(She had taken the secret shortcut.)

"I got chocolate Bucko Bammo Bars,"
she said, "with nuts!"
"Yummm…," said Mr. Green,
"my favorite."

Mrs. Green ate her bar slowly,

in 97 licks and 33 nibbles.

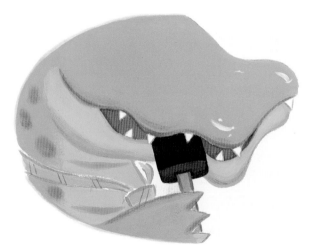

Mr. Green ate his bar quickly,

in 6 big sloppy bites.

(He finished first,

but it was not a race.)

Mr. Green was still hungry—
so was Mrs. Green.
"Let's go home and
make spaghetti," he said.
"With mashed potatoes!" she said.

Mrs. Green took Mr. Green's hand.

"And on the way home," she said,

"we might see a purple-spotted dragonfly."

"Or perhaps...," said Mr. Green,

"another ice-cream truck!"